Dracula Doesn't Rock and Roll

There are more books about the Bailey School Kids!
Have you read these adventures?

Dracula Doesn't Rock and Roll

by Debbie Dadey
and
Marcia Thornton Jones

illustrated by John Steven Gurney

A
LITTLE APPLE
PAPERBACK

SCHOLASTIC INC.
New York   Toronto   London   Auckland   Sydney
Mexico City   New Delhi   Hong Kong

ISBN 0-439-04399-9

Text copyright © 1999 by Marcia Thornton Jones and Debra S. Dadey.
Illustrations copyright © 1999 by Scholastic Inc.
SCHOLASTIC, LITTLE APPLE PAPERBACKS, THE ADVENTURES OF THE BAILEY SCHOOL KIDS, and associated logos are trademarks and/or registered trademarks of Scholastic Inc.

12 11 10 9 8 7 6 5 4 3 2 1   9/9 0 1 2 3 4/0

Printed in the U.S.A.   40

First Scholastic printing, November 1999

Contents

Dracula Doesn't
Rock and Roll

1

Coffin

"What a great day!" Melody sang and danced down the snow-covered sidewalk. She was walking down Delaware Boulevard after school with her friends Howie, Liza, and Eddie.

"Are you crazy?" Howie asked, looking up at the gray sky. "It's freezing out here."

Melody nodded, her black pigtails swinging beside her ears. "I know, isn't it great? I love winter."

Liza shivered and hugged her coat tighter as they neared the Clancy Estate. "Since when do you love winter?"

Eddie tried to scoop up a snowball but only got a few flakes in his glove. "What good is winter if you can't have a snowball fight?"

Liza giggled when she heard a rumbling sound. "Is your stomach growling again?" she asked Eddie.

Eddie pulled his baseball cap down to try to cover his red ears. "No, but I am hungry."

"You're always hungry lately," Howie told his friend.

Eddie shrugged. "My grandmother says I must be growing."

Liza's eyes got wide. "That noise is growing, too," she said. "And it sounds like it's coming from the Clancy Estate."

The kids stared at their teacher's home. It was a big, old house with broken shutters and cracked windows. The iron fence surrounding the yard was rusty and the open gate squeaked when the wind blew. Most kids at Bailey Elementary thought the Clancy Estate was haunted and that their teacher, Mrs. Jeepers, must be a vampire to live there.

Grrrm! Grrrm! "There it is again,"

Howie said, covering his ears. "That sound gives me the creeps."

"I think it's coming from the basement," Eddie told them.

"It sounds like someone is in terrible pain," Melody said with a gulp.

"Someone or something," Eddie said.

Liza stared at the dark windows of the house. "Maybe we should try to help."

"Are you kidding?" Eddie snapped. "Don't you remember what's in Mrs. Jeepers' basement?"

"I remember," Melody whispered, thinking back to the long wooden box that looked just like a coffin. The long box was locked from the inside and they were sure they had heard something moving inside it.

"Oh my gosh," Liza squealed. "What if that noise is someone trying to get out of the coffin?"

2

Burglar

"Let's go home and get a snack," Eddie suggested. "I bet my grandmother made cookies."

"But what about the noise?" Liza asked.

"Who cares?" Eddie said.

Liza put her hands on her hips. "Are you scared?"

Eddie shook his head. "I'm not scared of anything," he bragged.

"That proves you're crazy," Melody said. "There are some things you should be scared of, and creepy noises coming from basements are one of them."

Liza rubbed her mittens together to stay warm. "Do you think Mrs. Jeepers could be hurt in there?" she asked.

Howie shook his head. "No, Mrs. Jeepers always stays late at school to grade papers. It can't be her."

"Maybe it's a burglar caught in a trap," Melody suggested.

"Serves them right," Eddie said. "They shouldn't be stealing from Mrs. Jeepers."

Liza nodded. "Stealing is wrong," she agreed, "but nobody should have to suffer. Maybe we should look in the window and check it out. Then we could go back to school and tell Mrs. Jeepers about it."

Melody groaned. "I don't think this is such a good idea, but I guess it wouldn't hurt to look." The four kids pushed past the squeaky iron gate and over the frozen grass. They edged closer and closer to the basement window.

Argggghhh! Errrrrkkkkk! The noise got louder and louder. Liza put her hands over her ears. "What a horrible sound," she said.

"It sounds like a monster," Howie whispered.

The kids were almost close enough to

touch the basement window. One of the glass panes in the window was cracked and the other was completely missing. A piece of cardboard covered the empty spot.

Melody gulped and looked at Eddie. "You look first," she said.

"Me?" Eddie squeaked. "Why me?"

"Because you said you weren't afraid of anything," Howie whispered.

Eddie pulled his baseball cap down tighter over his head and wished he wasn't such a bragger. He stepped closer to the window.

EEEEEEEEKKKKKKK! A screech blasted out of the basement window. It was so loud the kids thought their ears were going to explode. Liza screamed, "RUN!"

3

Winterfest

Melody, Howie, and Eddie watched Liza sprint down Delaware Boulevard and dodge behind a clump of bushes.

"Liza's imagination is getting the best of her," Melody said, but she didn't sound like she believed it.

Just then a steady pounding like the sound of a monster's heartbeat started. It began slowly and then picked up speed until Howie's teeth rattled. Suddenly a high-pitched squawk erupted from the basement, sending goose bumps racing up Eddie's arms.

"Maybe Liza isn't so silly," Melody said with a shaking voice.

Howie nodded. "Let's get out of here!" he screamed.

Melody didn't wait for him to say it

twice. She raced down the street with Howie. Eddie took one last look at the basement door and hurried after his friends. They jumped over the bushes and landed right next to Liza.

"Smooth move," Eddie told his friends once he caught his breath. "If it was burglars, they know we're out here now."

Liza whimpered and looked up into the darkening sky. "What if it isn't burglars?" she asked. "What if it's vampires

beating their wings, getting ready to swoop over Bailey City?"

"Maybe the noise was a puppy dog trying to find some doggy bones," Eddie argued.

"Then the puppy must be the size of a dragon, and the only bones it'll be looking for are the kind that belong to kids," Melody told him. She poked Eddie's arm to prove her point.

"We have to run back to school and tell Mrs. Jeepers before whatever is down there destroys her basement," Liza said.

"We could go home and call the police," Howie suggested.

Eddie shook his head. "We don't have to go anywhere because there's Mrs. Jeepers now."

Mrs. Jeepers was bundled up in a long black cape with shiny black polka dots. Her cape kept getting swept back by the cold winter wind, like huge bat wings. Her black pointy-toed boots kicked up

12

the snow as she walked down Delaware Boulevard. The only thing that wasn't black was her red hair tied back with a black-and-yellow polka-dotted ribbon.

Liza waited until Mrs. Jeepers was almost to their hiding place before jumping from behind the bush. "We have to warn you," Liza blurted. "You can't go home!"

Melody, Howie, and Eddie pushed their way through the bushes and nodded. "There's something terribly wrong," Melody added.

Mrs. Jeepers remained calm as the kids explained the strange goings-on in her basement. When they got to the part about the noises, Eddie did his best to make the sounds himself, but Mrs. Jeepers gently rubbed her brooch and Eddie got quiet immediately. The kids were pretty sure that the mysterious green pin Mrs. Jeepers always wore had some kind of magic that made kids behave.

Finally, the kids finished telling their teacher about the strange noises, but Mrs. Jeepers didn't seem upset at all.

"I am so glad you enjoyed the BATs," she said in her strange Transylvanian accent. "They are using my basement to practice for the Winterfest."

She smiled her odd little half smile and added, "You are just going to die when they perform!"

4

BATs

"I don't want to die," Liza moaned the next day before school.

Howie, Melody, and Eddie had met her under the oak tree on the school's playground. At least three inches of snow layered all the branches, and icicles hung from the nearby swing set. Eddie was busy stomping a path in the snow around the giant tree. He acted like he wasn't listening to a single word anyone was saying.

"Nobody's going to die," Howie said, patting Liza on the shoulder.

"But Mrs. Jeepers said we would die when the BATs performed at the Winterfest," Liza whimpered.

Every winter the city had a big celebration in the gymnasium of Bailey

School. This year's Winterfest was just two days away.

"Don't worry," Howie told her. "We don't even know what BATs means."

"If it's a secret only Mrs. Jeepers knows about, then it must be bad," Liza said with a shiver.

"We don't know that for sure," Howie said. "Once we find out what BATs stands for I'm sure everything will be fine."

"I know all about bats," Eddie said. "They're what you use to slam baseballs out of the field."

"I don't think that's the kind of bats Mrs. Jeepers is hiding in her basement," Liza said.

"There is only one kind of bat our vampire teacher would protect," Melody said, "and that's the kind with wings! We only have two days left until Winterfest, and for all we know Mrs. Jeepers just brought her vampire buddies to a two-thousand-year reunion."

"Do vampires have reunions?" Eddie asked.

Melody jabbed him on the arm. Eddie stumbled and fell back against the tree. When he did, a pile of snow fell from the branches above and landed right on his head.

"How would I know?" Melody asked. "Do I look like a vampire?"

"No," Howie whispered, "but *he* does."

Melody, Liza, and Eddie looked where Howie pointed. A man dressed in black floated from shadow to shadow, being careful not to walk on the sidewalk where the winter sun shone brightly on the ground. He wore a long black coat that dragged through the snow. Its collar was pulled up high, and a big black cowboy hat cast his face in deep shadows.

The man acted like he didn't want to be seen. He looked up and down the street before hurrying across the school's parking lot. Then he pulled open the door to

Bailey Elementary School and slipped inside.

"Who was that?" Eddie asked.

Melody scratched her head with a gloved hand. "He reminded me of someone," she said.

Howie nodded. "Me too," he said. "And it's someone straight out of a horror movie!"

5

Mr. Drake

Liza shivered as the bell rang and the kids walked toward the school. "I just hope that guy doesn't go near the third grade. He gave me the creeps."

But Liza wasn't so lucky. When they entered their classroom the tall stranger in black stood in front of the blackboard, whispering to their teacher, Mrs. Jeepers. Melody gulped. "Maybe they're planning a vampire reunion right now."

"Don't you know who that is?" Howie whispered as he sat down at his desk.

Melody shook her head, but Liza spoke up. "That's Mr. Drake, our old school counselor."

"You mean Count Dracula," Eddie said.

The four kids remembered when Mr. Drake had been Bailey School's counselor. His office was as dark as a cave and he was always drinking pink lemonade. Some kids were sure he was the most famous vampire of all — Dracula.

Liza took out a pencil and sheet of paper to copy the spelling words from the board. "Eddie," she said softly, "we shouldn't call Mr. Drake names. He's probably just a very nice school counselor."

"Counselor, my eyeball," Eddie snapped. "His office looked more like a cave, and I bet he's from Transylvania, just like Mrs. Jeepers. You know what that means."

"Just because someone is from Transylvania, it doesn't mean he or she is a vampire," Melody said.

"No," Howie admitted, "but just look at him. You have to admit he doesn't look like an ordinary school counselor."

The four kids stared at Mr. Drake. He held a huge black case in one hand and a glass of pink lemonade in the other.

23

Mrs. Jeepers smiled and pointed to the case several times. Mr. Drake smiled, showing his pointy eyeteeth, and Mrs. Jeepers clapped her hands. "Class," Mrs. Jeepers said in her Transylvanian accent. "We have a special treat today."

Eddie groaned. "I hope my neck isn't the treat."

Mrs. Jeepers flashed her green eyes at Eddie and continued talking. "I am sure you remember Mr. Drake, our former school counselor. He is a member of the rock band that'll be making a special performance at this year's Winterfest."

"Performance?" Eddie whispered. "Is that what vampires call it when they suck your blood?"

Melody gulped as Mr. Drake sat the long black case on Mrs. Jeepers' desk. "Maybe he has his bat friends in that case," Melody said softly.

Liza sniffed. "I think my nose is going

to bleed." Sometimes Liza got a nose-bleed when she was upset.

"Don't bleed," Howie warned her. "Vampires go nuts at the sight of blood."

"Oh my gosh," Liza squealed. "He's opening the case."

6

Rock and Roll

Melody giggled. "It's only a guitar," she said with relief.

"I knew it all along," Eddie bragged.

"That's not just any guitar," Howie said. "It's an electric guitar."

Eddie's eyes got big. "Cool!"

Liza slumped down into her seat. "I'm just glad it's not a box of bats."

Mr. Drake's eyes swept around the room, looking at every student. Liza sunk even lower in her seat, but Melody sat up straight and raised her hand. "Mr. Drake," Melody said, "I thought Bailey City made you sick."

"Melody!" Mrs. Jeepers said, her hand touching her brooch.

Melody quickly continued. "I mean, I

thought you quit being a counselor here because of your allergies."

Mr. Drake licked his lips and smiled again. "You have a wonderful memory," Mr. Drake said in a hoarse accent. "My doctor has given me allergy medicine that allows me to live anywhere. Now I have a new career." When Mr. Drake smiled his eyeteeth flashed white.

Liza whimpered when she saw Mr. Drake's eyeteeth. "Modern medicine is just wonderful," Liza said.

Mr. Drake held up his electric guitar. It was bright red except for a black bat stenciled on one end. Mr. Drake strapped the guitar around his neck and plugged it into a big black box sitting on the floor.

BLAMMM! TWANG! TING! Liza held her hands over her ears. "He's not going to suck our blood," Liza whispered. "He's going to drive us insane with the noise."

"All tuned up," Mr. Drake said with a smile. "Who is ready to rock and roll?"

A few kids raised their hands uncertainly as Mr. Drake took a sip of pink lemonade and then continued. "This is a song I wrote. It is called 'Bailey City Rock.'"

Mr. Drake strummed his guitar and started singing. Melody couldn't believe it — it actually sounded good. Mr. Drake strummed and plucked and bent the strings on his guitar. His voice was deep and rough, and the beat of the song was fast. Melody looked around the classroom. Carey, Jake, and Huey stood in the aisle, clapping their hands. Liza tapped her toes. Even Howie sang along.

"Rock on, Bailey City, rock on!
When the sun goes down,
Have a rock-and-roll marathon!
Shake, rattle, and roll your bones,
Our beat warms your blood,
'Til the dark meets dawn!
Rock on, Bailey City, rock on!"

Melody turned around to see if Eddie was enjoying the song. Melody gasped. Eddie must have liked the music. He was hitting two pencils against his desk as if he were playing the drums. But that's not what worried Melody.

Eddie was staring straight ahead as if he were in a trance.

7

King of Rock and Roll

Eddie couldn't wait for school to be over. He never could. But after hearing Mr. Drake play his electric guitar Eddie was even more excited than usual to get out of class. All during math, he tapped his pencil to the beat of "Bailey City Rock." During science, he couldn't stop humming. Mrs. Jeepers flashed her green eyes at Eddie, but he didn't seem to notice.

"You better be quiet," Liza warned, "before Mrs. Jeepers gets really mad." Once Eddie had pushed his teacher too far by shooting spitballs. Mrs. Jeepers had taken Eddie out into the hall. None of the other kids knew what had happened but it must have been bad because Eddie refused to tell them. He never

wanted to make her that mad again, so he tried to be good until the bell finally rang.

"Mr. Drake's guitar is the coolest thing I've ever seen," Eddie told his friends when they got outside. As usual, Eddie, Howie, Melody, and Liza had met under the oak tree on the playground. The sun was shining and the snow sparkled like a field of diamonds. But Eddie didn't even notice.

"I want to start my own rock band," he said.

"Are you crazy?" Melody asked. "Your grandmother would never let you have a rock band."

Howie nodded. "Grandmothers usually like old-fashioned music like Elvis and the Beatles."

"The Beatles sound like some kind of bug," Liza said.

Eddie rolled his eyes. "A beetle is a bug, but the Beatles were only the most famous rock-and-roll band ever."

Liza shrugged. "Who knows, maybe Eddie could become famous, too."

"Yeah," Melody giggled. "Eddie has so many rocks in his head, he could be the next king of rock and roll."

"Very funny," Eddie said with a sneer. "But you wait and see. I'm going to be in a rock band so I can play an electric guitar just like Mr. Drake!" To prove his point, Eddie danced around the tree, pretending to play a guitar. He sang "Bailey City Rock" at the top of his lungs. It sounded more like he was screaming.

"Do you have to be so loud?" Liza asked, holding her fingers in her ears.

Eddie still pretended to play the guitar. "Everybody knows rock and roll is loud, loud, LOUD!" he screamed.

"I just don't understand why Mr. Drake would want to start a band," Howie said. "After all, he had a perfectly good job as a school counselor. It's a known fact that teachers, counselors, and principals can't stand loud noises. That's why

35

they're always trying to make Eddie be quiet."

"Are you kidding?" Eddie asked. "Just think how exciting being in a rock band could be. I bet Mr. Drake got tired of all that quiet boring stuff that happens in schools."

Liza sniffed. "Working in a school is exciting, too. After all, no two days are ever the same."

Eddie rolled his eyes. "I'll give you three good reasons why being in a band is better than working in a school," he said. Eddie held up one finger. "First of all, if the band makes it big Mr. Drake will be rich, rich, rich."

"That's a big *if*," Melody interrupted. "Most bands never earn a dime."

Eddie ignored her and held up another finger. "Second of all, he could get famous. Girls will love him."

"Is that why you want to start a rock band?" Liza teased. She batted her eyelashes at Eddie. Melody made kissy noises.

Eddie shook his head and raised another finger. "The third reason is that it would be *fun* and that's why I would want to do it."

"Don't you realize it takes hours and hours of practice for a band to be good?" Howie asked.

"Practice shmactice," Eddie blurted. "All I have to do is turn on the stage lights and start playing. Entire cities will be hypnotized by how good I am."

"That's it," Howie gasped. "I know why Mr. Drake came to Bailey City. And if I'm right, I know exactly what BATs stands for. Trouble!"

8

Vampire Feast

Howie slumped against the tree and slid to the ground. His face was as pale as the snow that covered the playground.

"What's wrong?" Melody asked Howie.

"Are you going to faint?" Liza asked.

Eddie picked up a handful of snow. "A little snow in his face should perk him up."

Liza grabbed Eddie's hand before he could rub the snow in Howie's face. "Maybe you should go for help instead," she suggested.

Howie shook his head sadly. "There's nobody who can help," he moaned. "We're doomed. All of us."

"What are you talking about?" Liza asked.

"Mr. Drake doesn't want to have a Win-

terfest," Howie explained. "He's planning a Vampire Feast."

"What does playing a guitar have to do with a vampire banquet?" Eddie wanted to know.

"I figured it all out," Howie said. "The BATs plan to lure everybody to the Winterfest. Once we're there, everyone will be seated in the gym. The lights will be turned down so low we won't be able to see our hands in front of our faces. That's when it will happen."

Liza nodded. "That's exactly how the Winterfest always happens," she said. "As soon as the lights are turned down the band starts playing music."

Howie dropped his voice to a whisper. His friends had to kneel in the snow just to hear him. "I'm not talking about music," Howie told them. "I'm talking about a trap. A trap set by vampires."

Melody gasped. "I think I understand. You think that when the lights are turned off Mr. Drake and his band of Dracula buddies will swoop down and slurp up all the blood in the city!"

"Exactly," Howie said.

"That's disgusting," Liza said.

"Besides," Melody said, "you never even proved Mr. Drake was Dracula."

"After all," Liza added, "Dracula doesn't rock and roll."

"Or does he?" Howie said. "We have to find out — and stop those rocking vampires!"

A cloud passed over the sun, casting the entire playground in shadows. Liza shivered and Melody zipped her coat all the way up to her chin. "You better not let Mr. Drake hear you talking about him," Liza warned. "You might hurt his feelings."

"I don't want to hurt his feelings," Howie agreed. "I don't want anybody to get hurt. That's why we have to do something."

9

Bloodmobile

"I want to rock and roll all night!" Eddie screeched the next morning as Liza, Melody, and Howie walked up to him on the playground. It was cold and the snow on the ground crunched under their feet, but it wasn't loud enough to drown out Eddie's singing.

Eddie grinned at his friends. "I have a plan," he said. "If I save my allowance for the rest of this year, I'll probably have enough money to buy a used guitar."

"Why don't you just ask for one for Christmas?" Liza asked.

Eddie slapped Liza on the back. "You're a genius," he told her. "My grandmother is always trying to get me to play an instrument. I bet she'd love to buy me a guitar."

"I have a plan, too," Melody told her friends.

"Great," Eddie said. "You get the drums and we can start jamming."

Melody shook her head. "I'm not talking about drums and guitars. I'm talking about saving us from Mr. Drake."

"Oh, brother," Eddie groaned. "Not that again."

Melody gave Eddie a look that would break guitar strings. "This is important."

"Okay," Howie said. "Just tell us your plan."

"We'll give Mr. Drake exactly what he wants," Melody explained.

Liza shrieked. "He can't have any of my blood! I'm too young for the blood-mobile."

"This isn't a bloodmobile," Eddie said with a snicker. "This is more like a bat-mobile."

"Let's just stay calm," Howie said, "and listen to what Melody has to say."

Melody looked at her friends seriously.

"The first thing we have to do is to make the BATs famous. Then they'll forget about us. They'll be too busy playing at concerts and signing autographs to think about draining all the blood from Bailey City."

Liza put her hands on her hips. "How are we going to do that?"

"Just think about the most famous person you know," Melody said. "How did they get famous?"

"He played basketball better than anyone in the entire world," Eddie said.

"Does Mr. Drake play basketball?" Liza asked.

Howie slapped his forehead and groaned. "Basketball is not the point."

"It is to me," Eddie snapped.

Melody stomped her foot on the frosty grass. "People get famous by advertising and that's what we have to do for Mr. Drake."

Howie snapped his fingers. "Good idea," he said. "If we let enough people

47

know about Mr. Drake's band he'll become so famous he'll leave Bailey City alone."

"And our necks," Liza said, rubbing her neck.

"Then we all agree," Howie said. "Let's do it!"

10

IT'S COMING!

Eddie stuck out his tongue as he finished painting the last letter of his sign. He held it up to show Liza and Howie. A little of the green paint dripped off the edge onto the kitchen floor, but the kids didn't notice.

Liza read the sign out loud. "'IT'S COMING!'" she read. "What does that mean?"

"Nobody will know what IT is," Howie added.

Eddie nodded. "That's right, so they'll all wonder. We have to get people interested and curious."

"Eddie makes sense," Liza said, picking up a paintbrush. She made neat letters on a piece of white poster board. IT'S COMING TO WINTERFEST.

"But we have to get everyone talking

about the band," Howie said, "and we can't do that if they don't know their name."

Liza nodded. "I've got it," she said. She dipped her brush in the red paint. She added BATS to the top of each sign. The dripping paint looked like blood.

Soon Howie, Liza, and Eddie had a pile of BATS . . . IT'S COMING signs stacked on Melody's kitchen table. "Why are we doing all this work?" Eddie complained. "This is all Melody's idea and she's not even helping."

"Where is she anyway?" Liza asked.

Howie pointed toward the hall. "She's in the family room making phone calls to tell people about Mr. Drake's band."

"Who is she calling?" Eddie asked.

Howie shrugged. "She wouldn't tell."

"Whoever it is, I hope she asked her mother first," Liza said. "She could get in big trouble."

Melody rushed into the kitchen full of smiles. "Okay, I'm done. Let's go hang up the posters."

The four friends taped posters up all around the library, Burger Doodle, and Bailey School. Kids stopped playing on the playground to read the signs.

"What's BATs?" a kid named Nick asked.

A boy named Jake shrugged. "BATs must be a new store in town."

A girl named Carey shook her head, making her blond curls swing. "You guys don't know anything. My dad told me that there's a new restaurant opening that's going to put Bailey City on the map."

"You're both wrong," Eddie told them.

"Then what is BATs?" Nick asked again.

Eddie grinned. "You'll have to wait until Winterfest. Tell all your friends and parents about BATs."

Melody, Liza, Howie, and Eddie walked home from the playground. "I hope this works," Liza said.

"It better work. The Winterfest is to-morrow," Melody said. "This is our only chance."

11

Vampire Dropouts

"Look," Melody squealed in the school gym at the Winterfest. "There's that WMTJ reporter. She is so good-looking."

Liza nodded. "And smart, too. If she likes the BATs, everybody will like them."

The reporter stood beside Mr. Drake. The kids listened as the cameras recorded her. "We're reporting live from the Bailey School gym. We've just found out the meaning of the mysterious signs popping up all over the city." The reporter held up one of the IT'S COMING signs. "IT is a sensational new rock band called the BATs. What exactly does BATs stand for?" the reporter asked and held the microphone in front of Mr. Drake.

Howie, Melody, Liza, and Eddie held

their breaths. Mr. Drake sucked pink lemonade through a straw before answering. Then he smiled so big the kids saw his pointy eyeteeth from their seats across the room. "BATs," Mr. Drake said in his Transylvanian accent, "means we're the BEST ACT in TOWN!"

The reporter laughed. "We'll see if that's true. We're going to give the tri-state area a taste of your music right after these messages from our sponsors."

The cameras went dead and Liza jumped up and down. "We did it! We did it!" she shouted. "The BATs are going to be famous."

Several parents stared at Liza. Melody put her finger to her lips. "Be quiet," Melody said. "We haven't done anything yet."

"But the gym is full," Eddie told her. "I've never seen so many people at the Winterfest."

"Oh, no," Howie said. "Once Bailey City gets a look at this band we can forget about them being famous." Howie pointed to the band.

The kids stared at Mr. Drake's band. They were definitely not dressed like most of the people in Bailey City. Two of the men had long hair that stuck out as if they'd been electrocuted. One man had shaved his head and had a tattoo on his arm. A woman in the band had bright red hair with black lips. All of the BATs were dressed completely in black. Every band member had a glass of pink lemonade sitting beside them.

"They look more like a band of vampire school dropouts than a rock band," Eddie admitted.

Liza clapped her hands. "I know what we could do," she said. "We could run home and get them nice cheerful clothes to wear."

"It's too late," Melody said. "They're already tuning up."

Liza covered her ears and took a seat. The gym was full of folding chairs facing

the BATs' stage. Eddie, Melody, and Howie took seats beside Liza, but not before noticing that lots of other people in the gym had their hands over their ears, too. "It doesn't look good for the BATs," Howie said sadly.

"And that's bad news for us," Melody added. "We're sitting ducks in a vampire arcade."

The lights in the gym went dim and Liza whimpered. Without even thinking about it Liza, Melody, Howie, and Eddie all put their hands over their necks as the band started playing.

The parents in front of Melody stared in silence. So did the people beside Eddie. "I don't think they like it," Eddie told his friends.

"They hate it. We're doomed. We'll never get rid of Mr. Drake now," Liza moaned as the band finished their first song. Then Mr. Drake hit a loud chord on his guitar. The rest of the band joined in as Mr. Drake sang, "Rock on, Bailey City, rock on!"

"Now look," Howie whispered. The kids looked around. The other students and even their parents smiled. Two fourth graders banged their hands on the seats in front of them and Eddie pretended to play the guitar. All around them people clapped to the beat.

Melody saw the cameras from WMTJ recording the people dancing in the aisles. Pretty soon, everyone was up and

dancing. Even Liza, Melody, and Howie clapped their hands. Howie saw Mrs. Jeepers dancing with Principal Davis. The camera got them all on television.

Eddie was having a great time. He twirled around in his chair. He sang every line as loud as he could but he still couldn't drown out the BATs. They were so loud the floor shook.

When the BATs finished "Bailey City Rock" everyone cheered for more. The BATs played song after song. The crowd

loved them all. When the band ended the concert the crowd yelled for them to keep playing, but a woman in a green bodysuit and purple hair whisked the BATs off the stage.

"I wonder who that is?" Melody asked.

Liza breathed a sigh of relief. "I don't care if she's the president of Timbuktu. I'm just glad she took them away before they bit my neck."

"We're safe," Howie agreed. "At least until we find out if our plan worked."

"It has to work," Melody said softly, "or we're in big trouble. Vampire trouble!"

12

Bailey City Monster

Liza and Melody watched Eddie swinging from the branch of the oak tree the next morning. Eddie was singing "Bailey City Rock" at the top of his lungs when Howie rushed up.

Howie shook the newspaper in his hands to get his friends' attention. "Look what I found in the paper!" Howie shouted over Eddie's singing. "It made the front page!"

Eddie jumped down from the tree's branch. "I have news, too," Eddie said. "I want to be the first to tell."

Melody, Liza, and Howie crowded around Eddie. "Did your grandmother buy you an electric guitar?" Melody asked.

Eddie shook his head. "She said I had

to learn to play piano before I could get a guitar. But I came up with another plan!"

"What is it?" Liza asked.

Eddie stood up tall and puffed out his chest. "I decided to join the BATs!" he told them.

"No. You can't," Howie said.

"Howie's right," Melody told Eddie. "Mr. Drake and his batty musicians would never let a kid join their band."

"You don't know that for sure," Eddie snapped. "I'm going to ask Mr. Drake this afternoon and I bet he'll say yes."

Howie shook his head. "You're wrong," he told Eddie. "Because Mr. Drake isn't even in Bailey City!"

"What do you mean?" Eddie asked.

"It's all in here," Howie said, pointing to the newspaper. "Right on the front page."

"Let me see that," Eddie said and snatched the paper from Howie's hand. He held it up so all the kids could see the headlines. "'BATs GO ON TOUR,'" Eddie read out loud. "BATs proved their name was true last night at the Bailey City Winterfest. They really were the BEST ACT in TOWN!"

Howie nodded. "The rest of the article explains everything. That lady with the purple hair was the manager for the Dead Beats. They want the BATs to open for them."

"Wow!" Eddie said. "The Dead Beats are the hottest band around."

"Then we did it," Melody said with a grin. "We helped make the BATs famous."

"And we got them to leave town before they drained us dry," Liza said. "We're safe from Dracula!"

"All that vampire talk went to your heads," Eddie told her. "Mr. Drake isn't Dracula, he's a famous rock-and-roll guitar player, and I'm going to be just like him!"

To prove his point, Eddie started

singing at the top of his lungs. He jumped and hopped and wiggled his hips in time to his song.

Howie laughed. "Dracula might not rock and roll, but there is one Bailey City monster left who has rocks in his head," he said. "And his name is Eddie!"

Debbie Dadey and Marcia Thornton Jones have fun writing stories together. When they both worked at an elementary school in Lexington, Kentucky, Debbie was the school librarian and Marcia was a teacher. During their lunch break in the school cafeteria, they came up with the idea of the Bailey School kids.

Recently Debbie and her family moved to Aurora, Illinois. Marcia and her husband still live in Kentucky where she continues to teach. How do these authors still write together? They talk on the phone and use computers and fax machines!

reepy, weird, wacky, and
unny things happen to
he Bailey School Kids!™
ollect and read them all!

THE
BAILEY SCHOOL KIDS®

The Adventures of THE BAILEY SCHOOL KIDS®

- ❏ BAS0-590-25783-8 **#28** **Unicorns Don't Give Sleigh Rides** $3.50
- ❏ BAS0-590-25804-4 **#29** **Knights Don't Teach Piano** $3.99
- ❏ BAS0-590-25809-5 **#30** **Hercules Doesn't Pull Teeth** $3.50
- ❏ BAS0-590-25819-2 **#31** **Ghouls Don't Scoop Ice Cream** $3.50
- ❏ BAS0-590-18982-4 **#32** **Phantoms Don't Drive Sports Cars** $3.50
- ❏ BAS0-590-18983-2 **#33** **Giants Don't Go Snowboarding** $3.99
- ❏ BAS0-590-18984-0 **#34** **Frankenstein Doesn't Slam Hockey Pucks** .$3.99
- ❏ BAS0-590-18985-9 **#35** **Trolls Don't Ride Roller Coasters** $3.99
- ❏ BAS0-590-18986-7 **#36** **Wolfmen Don't Hula Dance** $3.99

- ❏ BAS0-590-99552-9   **Bailey School Kids Joke Book** $3.50
- ❏ BAS0-590-88134-5   **Bailey School Kids Super Special #1:**
    Mrs. Jeepers Is Missing! $4.99
- ❏ BAS0-590-21243-5   **Bailey School Kids Super Special #2:**
    Mrs. Jeepers' Batty Vacation $4.99
- ❏ BAS0-590-11712-2   **Bailey School Kids Super Special #3:**
    Mrs. Jeepers' Secret Cave $4.99
- ❏ BAS0-439-04396-4   **Bailey School Kids Super Special #4:**
    Mrs. Jeepers in Outer Space $4.99

Available wherever you buy books, or use this order form

Scholastic Inc., P.O. Box 7502, Jefferson City, MO 65102

Please send me the books I have checked above. I am enclosing $\_\_\_\_\_$ (please add $2.00 to cover shipping and handling). Send check or money order — no cash or C.O.D.s please.

Name $_____$

Address $_____$

City $_____$ State/Zip $_____$

T